SCOUT'S

BEST DAY EVER !

WORDS & PICTURES
JENNIFER FARLEY

THE O'BRIEN PRESS
DUBLIN

This is Scout.

This is cat.

Scout *loves* cat.

Cat loves ignoring Scout.

Scout, Daisy and Dad are going on a holiday around Ireland. Cat is staying at home with Gran.

Happy holiday dog

Cork City   Post Card

Hey Cat!

First day of the holiday and we are in the big city! There are some pretty fancy dogs here. I am fitting right in.

We met some buskers and I sang the songs of my people.

Best Day Ever!
your pal Scout x

Howling in the street dogs

Posh-shop shopping dogs

Fetching the ball dog

6

Thomond Park,
Limerick

Dearest Cat,
Today we cheered on the team.
Dad shouted at the ref and Daisy giggled.
I ran on the pitch and Dad shouted
at ME! I don't mind though, because
I got a new toy! Best Day Ever!
your buddy, Scout x.
p.s. I think the team want me to join them.

Crazy pitch invading dog!

€10

€2·50

€7·50

Sniffing at the
butcher's dog

Kilkenny

Dearest Cat,
We went to the castle this morning.

Then we had sausages for breakfast.
Best Day Ever! Delicious.

Dad seemed a bit tense.

your buddy, Scout x.

Running through the market dog

County Wicklow

Post Card

Hi Cat,
Today we climbed the "Sugar Loaf".
I couldn't find any sugar, but the
smells from the top were amazing.
I didnt realise how high the
mountain was and I felt a little dizzy!
Today was my first time in a
helicopter.
Best Day Ever! X Scout

Hiking up the hill dog

Brave mountain rescue dog

Bringing home the sheep dogs

Country Fair, Midlands

Dear Cat!
Today I hung out with the sheepdogs.
Did you know that more than one sheep are
called sheep and not sheeps?
Daisy put me in a competition called
"who is a good boy?" Guess who won?
Later, to celebrate, I rolled in
something really smelly. It was heaven!
Without a doubt, Best Day Ever!

your favourite good boy, Scout x

Putting on a show dogs

Meanwhile, back at home with Gran ...
Cat gets the postcards.

Archaeological dig dog

Lough Crew, Meath

Post Card

Dear Cat!
Today we went back in time! Daisy said
this tomb is older than the pyramids. There are
drawings on the walls.
I found a bone, but Dad made me put it
back. Apart from that it was the
Best Day Ever!

your bud, Scout x

Ancient tomb art dog

Trinity College Dublin

Post Card

5

Hi Cat!
We visited the Book of Kells today.
There are loads of pictures of dogs in it. Dad said
they are illuminated.
I found out that I can study to be a Dogtor
here too. Wow! Best Day Ever!

X Scout (Future DOGTOR)
P.S I will perform an operation on you
when I get back.

Clever-clogs college dogs
Helping across the road dog

Giant Celtic hound dog

Post Card

Giant's Causeway, Antrim

Dear Cat!

Somebody said something about a giant around here, but I've seen nothing. He wouldn't scare me anyway.

Best Day Ever!
Scout The Great x

Skipping across the rocks dog

21

Waiting for the boats dog

JONAH

Inishowen, Donegal

Hi Cat,

Hung out on the coast today.
Caught a fish and some crab for tea.
Best Day Ever!

You would have loved it.

Your best boy pal, Scout

Fisherman's best friend dog

Stalactite sniffing dog

Marble Arch Caves
Fermanagh

Hello Cat!
Today we went deep underground. It was
very dark. I think Dad was scared so I sat on
his lap. Best Day Ever.

your buddy, Scout x.
p.s. Did you know a stalactite hangs
down and a stalagmite points up?

Fearless fossil finding dog

Salthill, Galway

Hi Cat!
Today I dug some very deep holes.
Daisy built a castle.
We went swimming in the Atlantic Ocean. I dried
myself in some really stinky seaweed. It was HEAVEN.
Definitely the Best Day Ever!

Home soon. I've missed you. I bet you've
missed me too.

Friends Forever, Scout x

Swimming in the sea dog

Jumping off the pier dog

Did you miss me Cat?

Nope.

Did you miss me a tiny bit?

No.

Did you miss me a **teeny**, tiny bit?

Ok, maybe a teeny, tiny bit ...

Jennifer Farley is an author, illustrator and designer from Dublin. She lives in rural Ireland with her husband and two other hairy beasties called Otto and Juno.

Dedication
For Caroline, Deb and John

Acknowledgments
Huge thanks to O'Brien Press.
Ginormous thanks to Eoin O'Brien, editor extraordinaire.

First published 2021 by The O'Brien Press Ltd,
12 Terenure Road East, Rathgar, Dublin 6, D06 HD27, Ireland.
Tel: +353 1 4923333; Fax: +353 1 4922777
E-mail: books@obrien.ie
Website: www.obrien.ie
The O'Brien Press is a member of Publishing Ireland.

ISBN: 978-1-78849-174-7

7 6 5 4 3 2 1
25 24 23 22 21

Printed and bound in Poland by Białostockie Zakłady Graficzne S.A.
The paper in this book is produced using pulp from managed forests.

Published in

DUBLIN
UNESCO
City of Literature

Scout's Best Day Ever! receives financial assistance from the Arts Council